Tang

Noa

Draff

I'm Pablo!

Llama

Mouse   Wren

These are my friends, the Book Animals!
The Book Animals live in the Art World,
where I draw my stories.

One day, as a special treat, Mum took me
to the zoo.
Of course, all the Book Animals came, too!
"There are so many animals here," said
Wren. "It's amazing!"
"It's amazing," said Llama.

Some of the zoo animals were very
different to the Book Animals.
"Eeeek!" said Mouse.
"What's that?" asked Noasaurus.

"That is what is known as a **chameleon**," said Draff. "It can change the colour of its body to blend in with its surroundings, in point of fact."

Lionfish only use their stings for defence. If another animal threatens it, the lionfish does not need to swim away. It can simply point its deadly **spines** towards the enemy.

The lionfish's stripes warn predators to stay away.

Lionfish spread out their fins to catch prey.

Lionfish are hunters. They corner prey with their large fins before swallowing them in one gulp.

Reef sharks

With its wide jaws and jagged teeth, the reef shark is a fierce hunter. Most sharks have a slim body and a powerful tail fin, perfect for gliding through water.

Octopuses, crabs and sea snakes are just some of the animals hunted by reef sharks.

Reef sharks have rows of deadly, jagged teeth.

Large flaps of skin make it difficult to spot the wobbegong shark on the seabed.

Sharks, such as the large black-tip reef shark and the small wobbegong shark, swim up and down the reef, on the lookout for fish and squid. They often hide in caves during the day and come out at night to hunt.

Sea slugs

Most sea slugs are the same size as garden slugs, but others are longer than a person's arm! Their bright colours warn other animals that they taste horrible.

Sea slugs eat animals that do not move, such as sea anemones and **sponges**. When a sea slug eats an anemone, it keeps the anemone's stings and puts them on its own back for protection!

The sea slug feeds on coral reefs.

Sea slugs scrape food off the reef with their sharp teeth.

Sea slug eggs are laid in the shape of a coiled ribbon.

Giant clams

Two huge shells protect
the giant clam's soft body.
It cannot move, so stays in
the same spot on the reef.

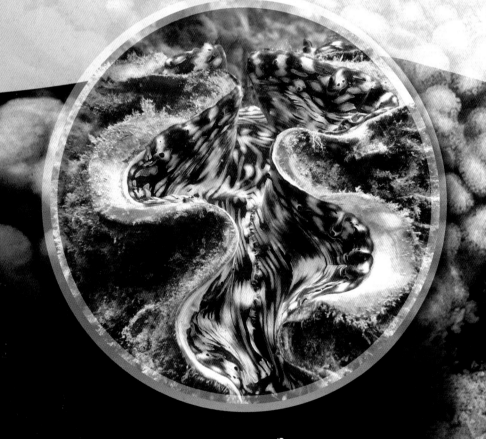

If a clam senses danger,
it quickly closes its shells.

and **chippety chip**
with the chisel.

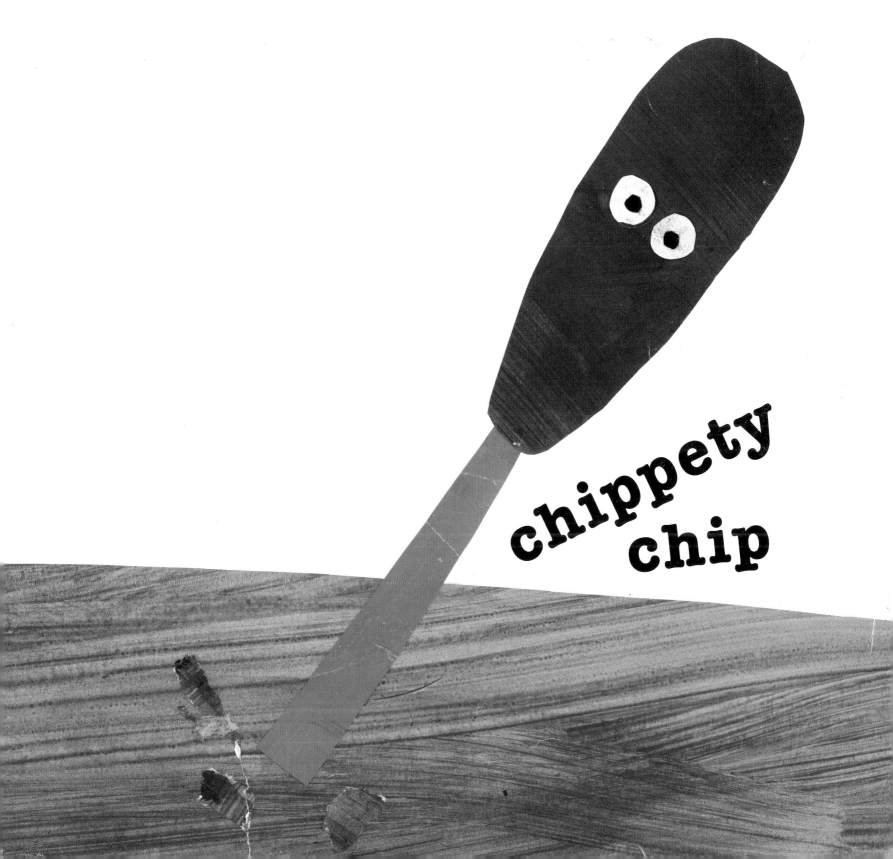

chippety
chip

We can **bang bang** with the hammer

and **t ppety t p** in the nails.

tappety **tap**

We can ▄▄▄ ▄▄▄ make a hole with the drill

and **twizzle** and **twist** with the screwdriver.

We can **twirl** the bolts

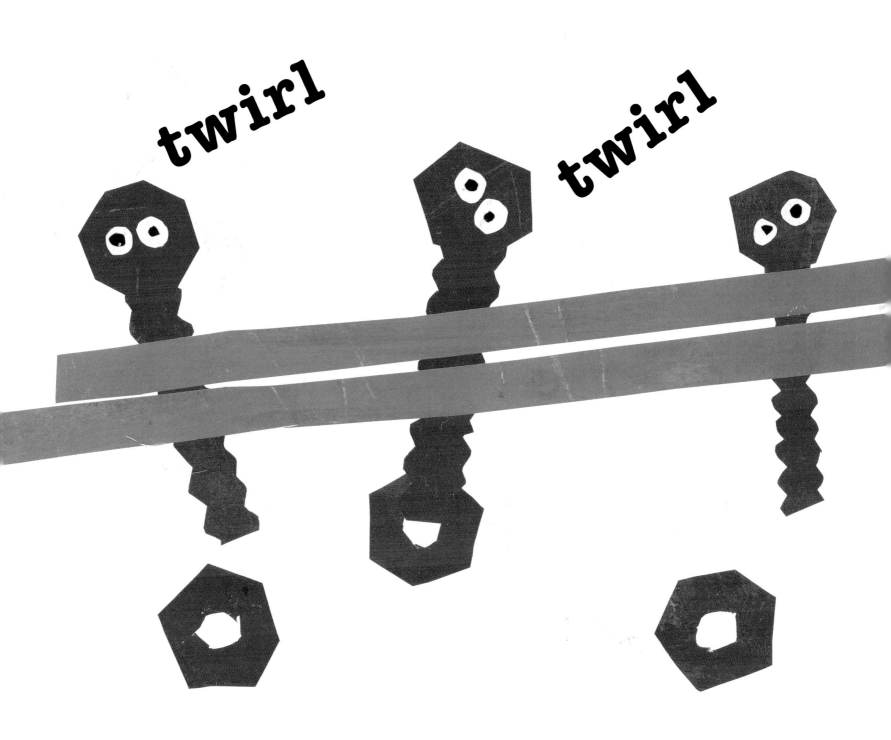

and **spin** the nuts.

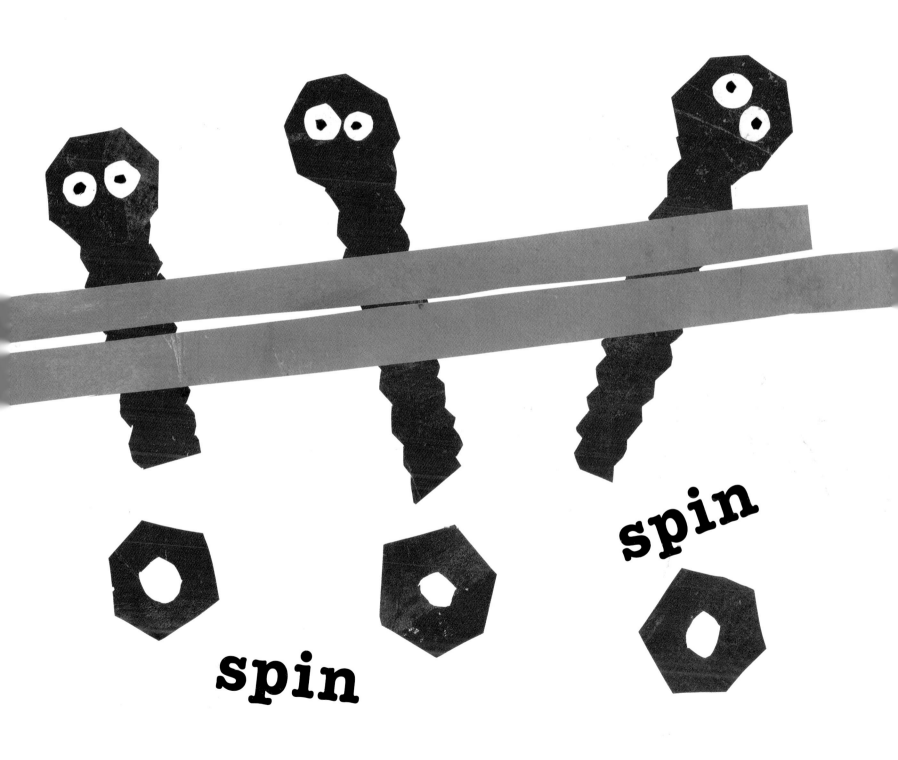

spin

spin

We can **grabbety grip**
with the pliers

grabbety
grip

and stickety stick
with the glue gun.

stickety
stick

We can **turn turn** with the spanner

and **clamp cl**amp tight
with the vice.

clamp
clamp

We can **ch ck chec** with the spirit level

check

check

check

and **measure** with the
tape measure.

 measure

measure

We can **whack whack**
with the mallet

whack
whack

and **lift lift** with the jack.

lift   **lift**

We can **rub rub**
with the sander

rub
rub

and **slap** and **slosh**
with the paintbrush.

slap

slosh

cree craw
cree craw

chippety
chip

bang bang

tappety
tap

zzz
zzz

twizzle

twirl

twist

spin

grabbety
grip

stickety
stick

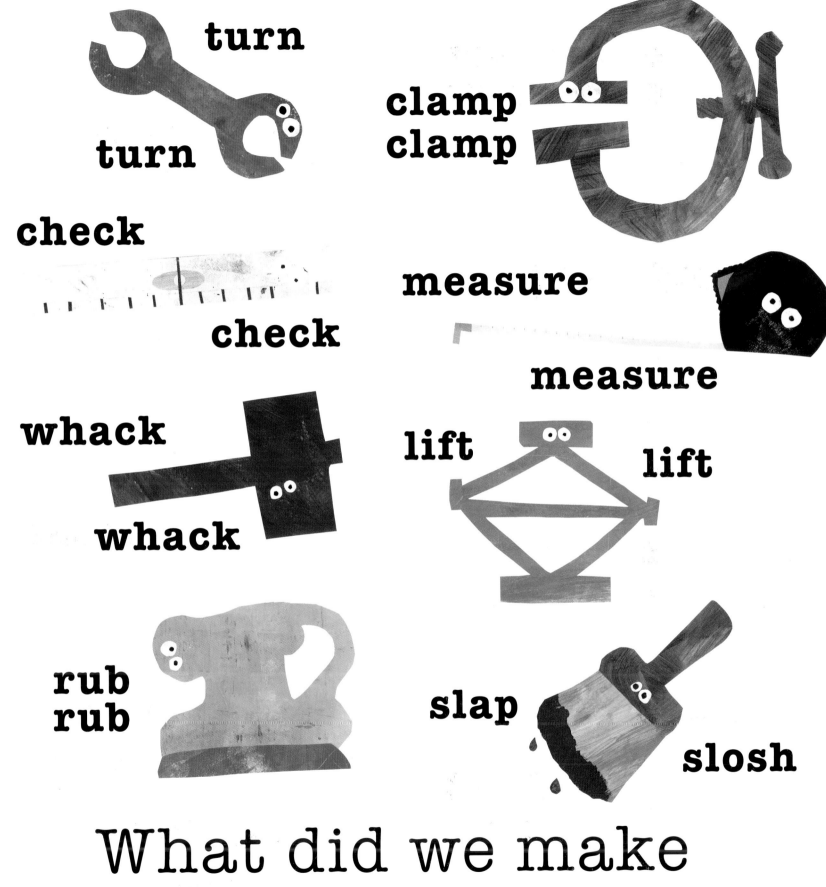

turn
turn

clamp
clamp

check
check

measure
measure

whack
whack

lift
lift

rub
rub

slap
slosh

What did we make
with all these tools?

We made a go-kart!

Now let's go, go, go!

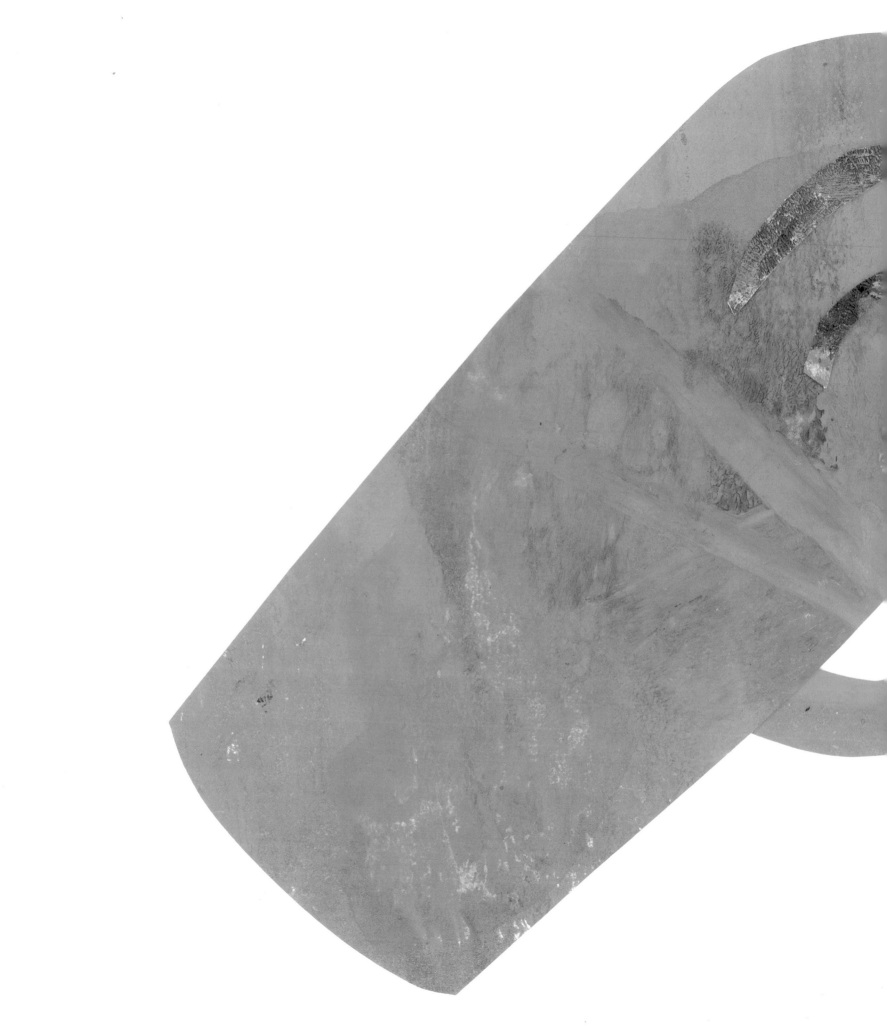

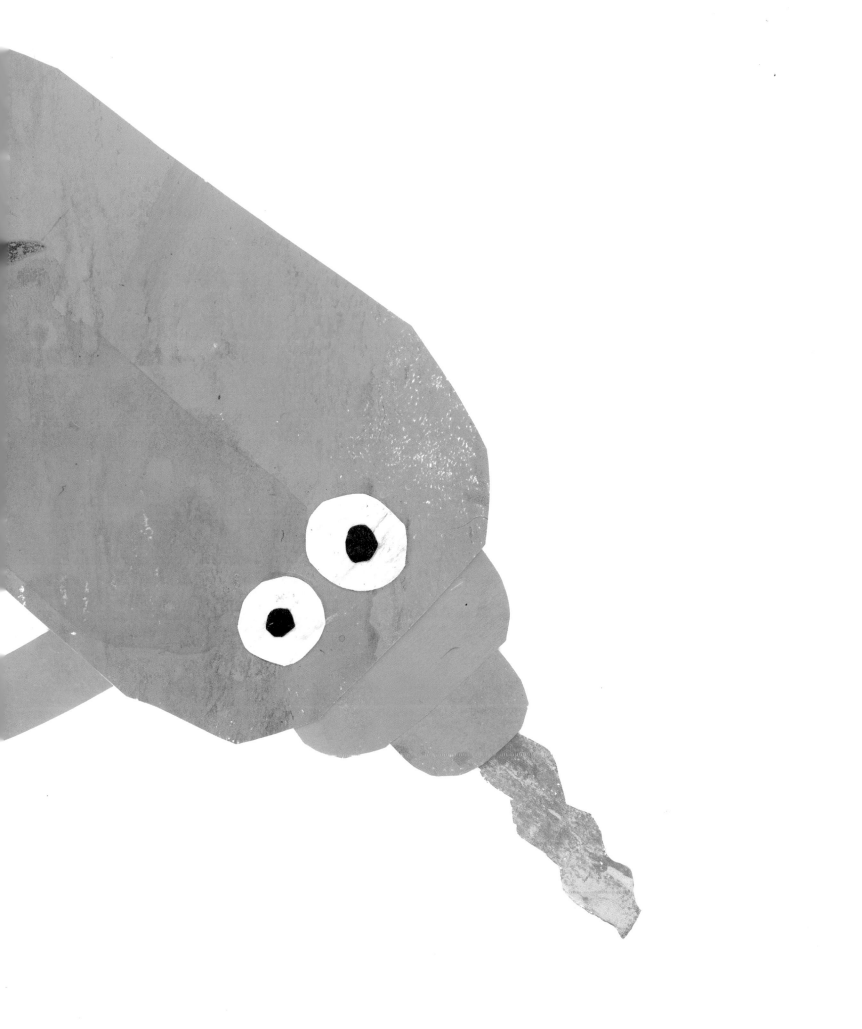

More Boxer Books paperbacks to enjoy

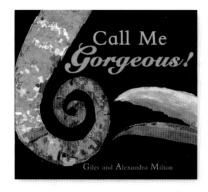

Call Me Gorgeous! • **Giles Milton & Alexandra Milton**

Discover a mysterious and fabulous creature in this beautiful book from Giles and Alexandra Milton. It has a porcupine's spines and a crocodile's teeth, a chameleon's tail and a cockerel's feet. What on earth could it be?

ISBN 978-1-907152-49-8

Meeow and the Pots and Pans • **Sebastien Braun**

Join in with Meeow and friends as they use objects from around the kitchen to make musical instruments. This bright, colourful book about creative play will inspire children to see what wonderful things they can do too!

ISBN 978-1-907152-50-4

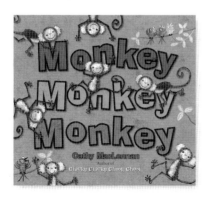

Monkey Monkey Monkey • **Cathy MacLennan**

Little Monkey explores the jungle, experiencing new sights and sounds and making friends along the way. But what Monkey really wants is monkey-monkey-monkey nuts! Where will he find some? Follow Monkey and find out! A rollicking rainforest romp, full of rhythm and energy.

ISBN 978-1-906250-73-7

www.boxerbooks.com